Skate Freak

Lesley Choyce

Orca currents

ORCA BOOK PUBLISHERS

Library and Archives Canada Cataloguing in Publication

Choyce, Lesley, 1951-

Skate Freak / written by Lesley Choyce.

(Orca currents)
ISBN 978-1-55469-043-5 (bound).—ISBN 978-1-55469-042-8 (pbk.)

I. Title. II. Series.
PS8555.H668S49 2008   jC813'.54   C2008-903218-7

Summary: Quinn Dorfman is struggling at school and is
watching his family deteriorate and, since moving to a new town,
has trouble enjoying his passion, skateboarding.

First published in the United States, 2008
Library of Congress Control Number: 2008929088

Orca Book Publishers gratefully acknowledges the support for its publishing
programs provided by the following agencies: the Government of Canada
through the Book Publishing Industry Development Program and the
Canada Council for the Arts, and the Province of British Columbia
through the BC Arts Council and the Book Publishing Tax Credit.

Cover design by Teresa Bubela
Cover photography by Getty Images

Orca Book Publishers
PO Box 5626, Station B
Victoria, BC Canada
V8R 6S4

Orca Book Publishers
PO Box 468
Custer, WA USA
98240-0468

www.orcabook.com
Printed and bound in Canada.
Printed on 100% PCW recycled paper.

11 10 09 08 • 4 3 2 1

For Jody

chapter one

If it's worth doing, do it. If it's not worth doing, do it anyway. That's my motto. It keeps me going.

Leaving Willis Harbor knocked the wind out of me. Moving to the city was not my idea. I liked my old hometown by the sea. I had lots of time to myself. I had the sea. I had my skateboard. I was the only skate-boarder in that small town. And I had the rocks, the Ledges, as they're called. At the

Ledges I pictured myself as the boy with wings. The Wingman.

That's not what they called me in the city. The guys I met at the skate park on the Commons tried out a whole lot of names on me. But the one that stuck was this: Freak. Skate Freak.

That first Friday afternoon it was crowded at the downtown skate park. Everybody knew each other. There were kids on Razors, rollerblades, mountain bikes, freewheelers and, of course, skateboards. The skaters ruled. The other kids were just in the way. And the skaters—well, some of them were good.

I'd never skated a real skate park, not a manmade one anyway. Back home, I had the main road, a paved roadside ditch, one church railing and—the big challenge—the Ledges. The city had half-pipes and railings just for skaters (unreal!) and more curved concrete than I'd ever seen. At least I'd found *something* about this ugly place that I liked.

Skateboarding always made me feel in groove, totally chilled and high-wired at the same time. At the skate park, though, I felt none of that. I slapped my board down, kicked for speed and dropped into the middle of the bowl. Way too many people were zigzagging crazy patterns back and forth. It was madness.

I was getting some nasty looks. But I couldn't leave, even though that was what those ugly staring faces said without one word. It was clear I was not liked. Was it the way I looked? Was it my hair? Or was it just me?

That's exactly what it was. It was me. I was new. I was not one of them. This is what they did here. Make the new guy feel like used toilet paper. Then flush him.

And flush they did.

I dropped down one side of the half-pipe and rolled up the other. I wasn't trying to impress anybody. Two guys looped around me on their boards, breathing down my neck—some kind of test. I decided to be cool and pretend nothing was happening. I had as much right to skate here as they did.

I had to kick my board up twice to keep from running into a couple of younger kids, barely rug rat graduates. They both shot me looks like they hated me. For what? I kept wondering.

For being alive, they seemed to say. But that was just in my head. I kept at it, smooth and easy, nothing fancy. I increased my speed so that I hit the lip of the half-pipe, almost got air but didn't, and then I drove for the bottom, angry enough that if I had run into someone, I wouldn't have cared.

From behind, someone finally spoke. "Hey, freak," were the words.

The guy on the bike who spoke the words slammed down on me. The front wheel of his bike landed on the backs of my ankles. I folded forward until my knees hit the ground. The rest of my carcass followed until my lips were kissing concrete.

And all I thought was, Man, I hope my board is okay.

I'm not saying it didn't hurt. It hurt a lot, especially where my forehead followed my lips into the relationship with the concrete.

I lay there trying to figure out which part of my body hurt the worst.

I decided it was my pride. Sure, my lips were bleeding and my head was scraped and hurting and the backs of my legs felt like—well, they felt like someone had landed a mountain bike on them.

And the guy on the bike was riding away. He never went down. He had used me like I was just another rock in an obstacle course. I saw the name on the back of his jacket: *Hodge*. What kind of name was that?

As I lay there trying to recover, I realized that people were laughing. And then a skater coming down the half-pipe was yelling at me. Actually, it wasn't one, but two. The second skater was coming from the opposite side.

I waited for the delivery, but it never came.

Both skaters swerved around me and continued on. They were good. I rolled left, grabbed my board and decided to limp home.

The Wingman had lost his wings. The boy who flew had been grounded.

chapter two

I had been at the new school—Jerome Randall High, or Random High as the kids called it—for almost a week. It's safe to say I didn't fit in. Willis Harbor was only an hour's drive away. But it was if I had come from another planet.

I had never been good at school. I could draw. I was good at that. But words on paper were not my thing, and numbers were not my friends. And teachers. Well, teachers either thought I was stupid or stubborn, or, worst of all, they felt sorry for me.

I had no ambition other than to skate for the rest of my life. Get on my board— which thankfully was not busted in the bike incident—and skate. Maybe make enough money to buy some new trucks and better wheels sometime. That was my ambition.

But there was one good thing about school. Only one: the girl I saw putting a skateboard into her locker.

She wasn't in any of my classes. I only saw her in the hallway. I wasn't one of those dudes who could walk up and say, "Hi, my name is Quinn Dorfman, but you can call me Dorf." Not for a second.

I was the kind that slinked around the hallway like a stalker. How pathetic is that?

My father had taught me no social skills at all in his considerable time of unemployment. My mother had given up on that too. And on us, I was beginning to think. After my old man was laid off and the unemployment money was running out, she had decided to go out west and get what she called "a real job." So if I was going to figure out how to meet this girl, I was on my own.

I was too shy to ask anyone who she was, so I just thought of her as Skateboard Locker Girl (SLG for short), which sounds incredibly lame, but that's what I called her.

After the skateboard accident, I was walking around school with a fat purple lip and a scab on my forehead that looked like a piece of pepperoni. The look added to my aura of loserness, I'm sure, but I didn't care. I thought I'd let my face heal a little before I tried to speak to SLG.

But she caught me watching her from down the hall. It was as if she could sense someone was staring at her. She turned. And smiled.

At least I think it was a smile. I'm not sure. It was an almost-smile at least.

But the bell rang right away, and she slammed her locker and fled.

SLG had long dark hair, dark eyes, a beautiful face and, oh yeah, she had a sweet custom skateboard from Homegrown Skateboards, one of my favorite board makers. I vowed that some day (after a bit of facial healing), I'd walk up to her and tell her straight out that I liked her board.

That's what I would do.

After school, I retrieved my own beat-up board from my locker and spit on the right front wheel for good luck. Some younger kids saw me, and I could tell I grossed them out.

"Sorry, dudes," I said, "it's what I do." As if that explained anything.

I don't like having to explain myself. I do what I do and I have my reasons.

Or not. But I do what I do anyway.

Outside, it smelled really funky. There was a brewery down the street and, well, it smelled like a brewery, I guess. As I cruised down the sidewalk on my board, I sniffed at the funky air, sang some of the lyrics from the Dead Lions song, "Garbageville," and I thought about Willis Harbor.

I didn't wear earbuds or have an Mp3 player in my pocket. I don't do that. I make my own soundtrack. I don't sing as well as Linus from Dead Lions, but I like hearing my own voice. I sing lyrics from my favorite bands: Dead Lions, Dope Cemetery, Crime of the Century, Skate Moms and Poorhouse. Sometimes the music is just in my head. And that's cool too. The songs remind me of my old life—the good old days.

Aside from skateboarding, home life in Willis Harbor had not been great. My father worked at a fish plant and my mother was a waitress at a restaurant that was busy in the summer and slow in the winter. Then the fish plant closed, and so did my father.

It was a crummy job, but once he lost it, he seemed to give up. My mother was making next to nothing in tips since summer was over. Then she saw the ad in the paper. It was for free training for women to operate heavy equipment—something to do with oil drilling or mining. But we'd have to move out west.

My father didn't want to move. And neither did I.

But I guess my mother did.

She left. I thought she was coming back, but that didn't happen.

My father's plan of action was really no plan at all. We'd move into the city and *something* would come of it. He thought there would be a good job for him in the city. Maybe he was thinking of getting a job at the brewery. Maybe he thought a job would just happen. Just jump up and bite him in the ass.

But it didn't.

Pretty soon the unemployment money would run out. Then my father would have to stop watching television twenty hours a day and get a job.

My after-school routine in the city was to skate the streets until dark. Then, sometimes, skate some more. I stayed away from the skate park though. The streets seemed safer. Cars I could understand. Territorial skate dudes I could not.

I found some good rails—at churches mainly. All the city churches had excellent railings. Many of them were empty during the week, so I could get a couple of amazing slides and grinds and move on before anyone hassled me.

Back in Willis Harbor, there was only one railing—at the church, of course. Reverend Darwin, a very religious black man from Ghana, saw me popping ollies and grinding down the handrail one day, and he came out to talk.

"How do you do that?" he asked.

"I see it in my head. Then I just do it," I said.

"It's very beautiful, this thing you do. Your parents must be quite proud."

"Huh?" I had been expecting him to yell at me.

"It's good to see a young man doing

something worthwhile with his life. Do you believe in God?"

"Yes," I answered to please the reverend. If it allowed me to do the only railing in town, I'd believe in God.

"Excellent," he said, patting me on the back. "Bless you."

Then he went back in the church. Willis Harbor was that kind of place.

In the city, I made the rounds of a half dozen churches after school each day until the Friday after the bike incident. I had still not made contact with SLG, though I almost got up the courage twice before turning into a wimp.

I was at the Baptist church near the brewery. Some people were inside practicing for a wedding. I should have just gone down the street to the Catholic church. But the Baptist rail had a sweeter slide.

I had just made my move down the rail and was planting myself back on the sidewalk with that satisfying *whack* of wheels hitting concrete, when the police car pulled up. An officer got out almost before the car stopped.

I swallowed hard.

"You know that's breaking the law, right?" the cop asked.

"Um," I said. I wasn't good at skill-testing questions.

"You've probably been warned before, right?"

"Not really," I murmured. "Back home..." I was going to explain about Reverend Darwin, but I didn't have a chance.

"I don't know where back home is," he said. "But in this city, damaging property like that is an offense."

"I wasn't trying to damage anything. Maybe I scraped a little paint off but–"

"I'd call that vandalism. That's what I'd call it."

The wedding party was on the steps now, staring at me as if I'd just murdered someone.

"I'm sorry," I said.

"You're lucky, you know that?" the cop said.

"I am?"

"Yeah, we just had this campaign shoved down our throats by the mayor. We're supposed to make the city more kid-friendly."

"Well, that sounds like a good thing," I stammered.

"For you. It means that I won't fine you this time. I won't take you in."

"Thanks," I said. I was trained to be polite when someone was giving me a break.

"But, I am going to confiscate your board," he added. And with that, he grabbed my skateboard, turned and got back into the police cruiser. "If you want it back, you have to come down to the station with a parent."

And he drove off.

With my board.

chapter three

My father was watching a rerun of *Who Wants to Be a Millionaire* when I walked into the dingy apartment. "C. The answer is C," he said to the TV screen.

"Dad?"

"Just a minute." He didn't look away from the screen.

I heard the contestant on TV answer, "D. Final answer."

"Sorry, the answer is C," the show's host said, and the audience sighed.

My father turned to me and said, "If that had been me, I would have won fifty thou."

"Dad, I need you to go to the police station with me."

"The police station?" he said, his voice rising in volume. "What did you do?"

"Nothing really."

"Must have been something."

"It was nothing. I was skating in front of a church. A cop came and lectured me. Then he took my board."

"Then why do we have to go to the police station?"

"To get my skateboard back. He said I need to bring a parent."

"Looks like I'm the only one available."

"That's what I was thinking. Can we go there now?" I was feeling naked without my board. I felt lost. Almost dizzy.

"No," he said. "I think maybe this is a good thing. Time to stop fooling around with kids' stuff like skateboarding and move on."

I thought about calling my mother's cell phone number, interrupting her in her heavy equipment class maybe. But I thought I might start crying if I heard her voice on the phone. I wished there was something I could do to pull my family back together. But I knew there was nothing I could do. Nothing at all. So I went into the kitchen and microwaved a slice of frozen pizza. It tasted like crap. I'd put it right up there as the number one worst piece of pizza I'd ever nuked. The worst I'd ever eaten. Maybe the worst piece of pizza on the planet.

Saturday morning. Six AM. This was not territory I was at all familiar with. Someone was shaking my shoulder.

I opened my eyes. My father was standing over me.

"Get up, Quinn."

I looked at him, looked around at my crummy room. Oh yeah, I had to say to myself every morning. I'm not in Willis Harbor anymore. My life is a disaster. I tried to focus on the clock. The number six on the clock confused me. "It's Saturday, right?"

"Right."

"I don't have to get up for school." I noticed then that my father had a jacket on. His hair was combed—that was totally weird.

"No, but you have to get your butt out of bed, get dressed and go down to the police station with me." He was smiling now. I hadn't seen my old man smile since before my mom left. I guess he felt sorry for me losing my board after all. This was more like the father I knew back in Willis Harbor.

I shot out of bed and scooped up yesterday's clothes from the floor.

The city was strangely likeable in the early morning. The streets were nearly empty. I was beginning to see some possibilities. We made it to the cop shop by six thirty.

My father was nervous. "We're here to

see about the boy's skateboard," he said to the tired man behind the desk.

"Skateboard?"

"Yesterday," I said. "He said I needed to come down with a parent."

"He who?"

"The police guy."

"You don't know his name?"

"He didn't tell me."

"You should've asked."

My father interjected, "It was only yesterday. Could you please help us find it?"

"Been a long night," the man said. He let out a sigh. "Okay. We got this room with bikes and skateboards. Let's go have a look."

We followed him down a hallway, and I could tell being in the police station made my father nervous. Me too. I guess we'd both watched too many cop shows on TV. The hallways seemed really dirty.

"Nice place you have here," my father said, trying to lighten things up.

The man laughed. "Janitor quit this week.

Chief can't seem to get his act together to hire someone."

He stopped and opened a door. Inside were about twenty bikes and a big pile of skateboards—must have been almost fifty. "Probably in there somewhere," he said to me.

Now, me and my board go way back. We were soul mates. I walked forward and grabbed the trucks, picked the board up in an instant. I felt the universe lock back into place. I could have grabbed any board there. I could have taken a really expensive board. But I didn't. I wanted *my* board back.

"Kids," the man said to my father. "I got one of my own. He's fifteen. Plays video games nonstop. Can't figure him out."

"I know what you mean," said my dad.

I was smiling from ear to ear. Both men shook their heads and laughed.

In the hallway, my dad asked the guy, "So, are you looking for a new janitor?"

"Bet your ass we are, why?"

"Can I apply for the job?"

"Can you start tomorrow?"

"Yeah, I can do that."

"We'll have to run a criminal check on you this week though. Is that okay?"

"No problem."

Outside, in the cool morning air, the world seemed a little brighter. The funky smell of the brewery wasn't present, and I thought I could smell the sweet salt air of the sea.

My father took me out for breakfast, and we both ate like pigs. Which was very cool.

"I always wanted to be a janitor," he said, after we'd shoveled eggs, home fries and bacon down. He was joking, but it was a good joke. Then he smiled at me like the father I knew when I was little. Back when things were great.

chapter four

The next day, I heard my father get up early again to go to his job at the police station. I lay there looking at the cracks in the ceiling when it clicked. *Sunday morning.* The skate park would be empty.

I shot out of bed and gathered yesterday's clothes, dressed and grabbed my board. I kissed my board, I was so pumped.

The skate park was beautiful. The air was cool, and there was no wind. The sun was low in the sky, and everything looked green and fresh. The smell of wet concrete was awesome. I thought I was alone. Then I heard the sound. Someone was in the bowl.

When I saw her, my heart stopped.

SLG came up out of the bowl and popped ever so slightly into the air, tagged her board with her hand, indy-style, and landed gracefully back down onto the arched wall of the bowl, making hardly a sound. She was alone.

She went up the other side and did it again. As gravity tugged her back to earth, her ponytail swished up in the air in a way that paralyzed me.

And then she leaped off her board, kicking it up into the air. She stood there staring at me. The frozen boy.

And then she skated over to the half-pipe and continued her run.

I rolled ever so cautiously up to the bowl she had just vacated. I dropped, went halfway up the slope and just kind of rolled around for a bit, afraid to try any tricks with her nearby.

I was trying to get up the nerve to skate beside her, to introduce myself. But as I finally made my first real attempt on the lip, there she was. Right there, looking at me. I tried to ollie over onto the flat, but I lost my board and it tumbled below. And so did I.

Ouch.

She looked down at me without sympathy.

"What are you doing here?" she asked. She didn't sound thrilled to see me.

"Trying to avoid the crowds," I answered, attempting to stand up and recover what was left of my dignity.

"I liked having the place all to myself," she said.

"Sorry."

"I got tired of all the agro guys during the week. Just not worth it."

"I know what you mean."

She stared some more.

"You want me to leave?" I asked, fully on my feet now. I grabbed my board and walked up the sloped side toward her.

"I dunno yet."

"That's cool." When it came to conversations with girls, I was not the sharpest tool in the shed.

"Got a name?"

"Quinn Dorfman. Dorf for short."

She laughed. "I'd change that if I were you. Sounds too much like Dork."

"I'm used to it. I don't mind."

"I'm Jasmine," she said.

"You're kidding," was my brilliant reply.

"Jazz, for short. You go to Random, right?"

"Yeah, I saw you too. You keep your board in your locker." I made a serious effort to take my foot out of my mouth.

"And you like to stare. I noticed."

"Sorry. I just thought..." I was going to say she was cute or pretty or beautiful, but I stopped myself. "I just thought you had a really hot board. Homegrown, right?"

"Yeah. It was a present. My grandmother bought it for me."

"Your grandmother skates?"

"My grandmother is dead now. And she didn't skate. But she understood that some things are important."

"Sorry."

"About what?"

"About your grammie being dead."

"How'd you know I called her Grammie?"

"I didn't. That's what I called my grand-mother. She's dead too."

"Sorry."

"S'okay. Wanna skate? Before the place gets crowded?"

"Sure."

And it's just about then that a guy likes to show his stuff. He likes to show off. It was rather predictable, but I couldn't help it. I ripped. And so did she. We had the place to ourselves for another forty-five minutes. The only problem was that she was as good as me. Maybe better. And she knew it.

Then we were invaded by a rat pack of younger kids. Dweebs and dweebites on little bikes and scooters and a couple of skateboarders with runny noses.

The scab eventually fell off my forehead, and my lip wasn't as puffy anymore. I still had bruises on the backs of my legs, but they didn't hurt that much. Ever since I met Jasmine, I started to feel a little better about school despite...well, despite everything else.

As I walked by her locker, I stopped and said hi to her.

"You're still stalking me?" she asked. But she was smiling.

I blushed immediately. I didn't know what to say.

"Just kidding," she said. "It's okay."

"How come you have rocks in your locker?" I asked.

"Because I like rocks. I collect them. I'm going to be a geologist."

"Oh. Well, that's cool." A geologist? SLG wanted to be a geologist?

She held out an amazing purple crystal. "This one is amethyst."

I held it in my hands and was dazzled by it.

"And this one is an agate." She showed me another rock, this one polished with an incredible design inside it. "My favorites are the geodes though," she said and lifted out another one.

"It's hollow."

"That's the cool part. On the outside, it looks like a dull, boring rock, but inside it's like a magical kingdom."

The hollow cavern inside the rock had a thousand little crystals. "I know where some really cool rocks are," I blurted out, trying to keep up my end of the conversation.

"You do?"

I handed her back the amethyst. "Well, they're not like this, but they are amazing. Really amazing."

"Can you take me there some time?"

"For sure. It's by the sea. The town

where I grew up. This place is a very special place."

"What are they?"

"Huh?"

"The rocks. What kind of rocks?"

"Um. Granite, I think. They say that the rocks are hundreds of millions of years old."

Jasmine laughed again. "Of course. Most rocks are really old. And they all have stories to tell if you can read them."

"You read rocks?"

"Yes," she said as the bell rang, and she put her rocks back into her locker.

"You must be really smart," I said.

"I am. I'm really smart."

I guess my face must have given away what I was thinking: How could a really smart girl ever be interested in a not-so-smart skate freak?

"Hey, it's not like an incurable disease or anything," she said. "I gotta get to chemistry. See ya."

I wandered off to English class, feeling

confused but happy. She said she'd go with me to Willis Harbor. To the Ledges. I'd ask my dad to drive. No. Better yet, we'd take the bus. I wouldn't even tell her what the rocks had to do with skateboarding. It would be a surprise. It would be golden.

The only thing I was good at in school was daydreaming. I couldn't concentrate in class. I had a hard time sitting still. My mind wandered. I pictured Jasmine and me on the rocks at Willis Harbor. I could see it so clearly. But I was beginning to worry that once she realized who I really was, she'd lose interest.

chapter five

My mother had not called for over two weeks. No e-mail, no phone call. Nothing. I tried calling her cell phone a couple of times, but she didn't answer. When I asked my dad about it, he said, "Let's not talk about it." And then he started to talk about it.

"Things haven't been all that great between your mother and me for a while now."

"I know. I'm sorry, Dad."

"Your mother's a good person. I think I disappointed her."

"I think I did too."

"Not you, Quinn. Me. I lost the job."

"It wasn't your fault."

"Well, I took it kind of hard. Seemed like I'd worked at that damn fish plant all those years, and I guess I figured I'd work there until I retired."

"But you have a job now."

"Well, now is a little late, isn't it?" You could tell he was mad at himself.

I wanted to say something to make him feel better. I wanted to help somehow, but I didn't know what to say.

He took a deep breath and changed the subject. "How's school?" he asked for the millionth time in my life. Why do parents keep asking that question?

"School's great," I lied. "I love it."

"I don't believe you."

"Well, at least there's a girl there."

"You have a girlfriend?" He was smiling now.

"I didn't say that."

"What's her name?"

"Jasmine."

"Her name is Jasmine?" He looked puzzled.

"Jazz for short."

"Oh." The name indicated a girl from a completely different world than the one my father knew. But I thought I'd distract him from his own worries if I told him more.

"She skates. And she's smart."

"Wow." And that was the end of the best father and son talk we'd had in a long, long while.

My mother must have sensed this, because she called later that night. It was midnight our time. My father answered, and I opened my bedroom door so I could hear his end of the conversation.

It lasted about twenty minutes and seemed pretty serious. When he hung up, I went down to talk to him.

"Why didn't you call me? I wanted to talk to her."

"She said she couldn't talk to you without crying, and she didn't want that. Your mother misses you. She told me to tell you that."

"How is she?"

"She's still training. But she's already working part-time. Some kind of bulldozer. Can you picture your mother driving a bulldozer?"

"Not really," I said. "Is she homesick?"

"Yes."

"Is she coming back?"

"I don't think so."

"Did you tell her about your job?"

He hung his head. "No. I didn't."

"Why not?"

He didn't answer. He looked sad and defeated. It was like an infectious disease. I felt sad and defeated too. I felt like my mother had rejected me. Me and my dad were just a couple of losers in a crummy apartment. I hadn't noticed the paint before now. It was the color of vomit.

The next day, sad had given way to mad. I was mad at my mother for moving away. But

I could see things from her point of view. I was also mad at the world. Sometimes you just get really angry about the way things are going. That was me.

I got called on in math class. I forget what the question was, but my answer was the usual: "I don't know."

"You're not even going to try?" Mr. Carmichael asked.

"No," I said.

"You're not going to get very far in life with that attitude," he lectured.

I wanted to say something mean. But I didn't. I sucked it up.

I had no intention of letting Jasmine see me like this, and I was avoiding her for once instead of trying to run into her. By noon I was fed up with school and split. There was really only one place I wanted to go—back to Willis Harbor. But I didn't have money for the bus.

Instead, I cruised down to the skate park. It was crowded with kids from nearby schools, but I didn't care. I dropped into the bowl and elbowed my way around the little kids for a bit. Then I went over to the half-pipe and pushed for as much air as I could get. Each trip up the curve was followed by a serious drop as I connected with the wall halfway down the slope.

The other kids must have seen the look on my face. They got out of my way.

I was still mad, but skating helped.

Just when I thought I had the half-pipe to myself, that creep on the mountain bike, Hodge, arrived. This time he was wearing sunglasses. Before I understood what was happening, he was shadowing my every move—on his bike.

The guy was good. Real good. I didn't think you could even do this stuff on a bike. But Hodge could. I didn't slack off, but I had to be careful. Each time I'd slide down, he was there alongside me. But as soon as we hit the top and got air, he seemed to be able to hang there a freaking second longer so that I had to watch as he came down behind me.

He was on my case, for sure. I couldn't see his eyes behind the shades, but I could tell this wasn't just playtime for him. I remembered what it felt like when he'd brought his wheel down on the backs of my legs. He hadn't been fooling around then. He was hoping to do some damage.

I should have taken the hint and split. The other kids had seen me making these excellent power moves. I'd made my mark. Time to move on.

But each time I tried to make my exit, the bike guy was in my path. He dogged my every move. Then, finally, as we both shot for the top lip, he picked up speed and launched himself even higher than before. I jammed my board on the top lip, hung for a split second and then dropped ahead of the bike. What I hadn't counted on was Hodge coming down over top of me.

He didn't land on me. He went over me. He sailed over me and landed in front of me.

One thing that bikes can do better than

skateboards is stop with control. I guess that's because they have brakes.

As Hodge landed on the flat at the bottom of the half-pipe, he skidded sideways with the brakes on. And planted himself there like a wall.

It all happened in an instant. Maybe if I had been watching from the sidelines, it all would have seemed innocent enough. Or it might have looked like my fault.

I did a full-metal body slam into Hodge and his bike. Hodge had braced himself and stuck his knee out. The knee connected first—right into my crotch. Then I spilled forward onto him and his bike, knocking him over.

More pain. Crotch. Elbow. Right foot twisted under the bike.

Hodge's sunglasses had not even been knocked off, but he removed them as I peeled myself off him and his bike. My skateboard had kept on going up the other side on its own. It now came back down and smashed into the bike. I reached for it as I tried to stand, one hand holding onto my groin. The pain was starting to subside.

Kids were laughing.

Hodge looked at his bike first, then at me. He wasn't laughing.

"You never hear of right of way?"

"It wasn't my fault," I said.

"Whose fault was it then?" Hodge countered.

Stupid game, I thought. I'm not going there. "Nobody's fault," I said. "Stuff happens."

I turned to limp away. And then he said that word again.

"Yo, Freak. Wait."

chapter six

I turned around. Hodge had his shades back on. He was sitting cross-legged on the concrete, smiling. I walked back to him.

"Quinn Dorfman is the name," I said.

"I'm William Hodge. William. Not Bill."

"So. Bill," I said, "you seem to be on my case. Is there a reason?"

"No reason." He flipped his shades up so he could look me in the eyes. "I just wanted to see what you're made of."

"And?"

"A-one skate freak. You don't back down."

"Back down from what?"

"A challenge. I like that." William Hodge had that kind of smile that told you he always felt in control. It was the kind of smile you'd never trust. We had an audience, of course, but they were on the sidelines. "And you're good. You game for the next level?"

"Next level of what?"

"What I do on two wheels, you do with four."

I looked puzzled, I'm sure. I mean, I couldn't exactly skateboard on grass or go as fast as a kid on a bike. But I was curious.

"Come on, Quinn. It's just a friendly challenge. I've done it a hundred times. I've just never found a skater willing to try it."

"Where do we do this challenge?"

"At my house."

"You got a half-pipe?"

"Nope. You'll see."

I was still skeptical. "What kind of surface?"

"Asphalt shingles. It's a piece of cake."

I hadn't planned on going back to school for the afternoon, but I didn't have any plans to get myself killed. William Hodge had awakened the maniac who lived in my brain. The true maniac who believed that almost anything was possible on a skateboard. The maniac who was certain he could defy gravity, skate up the side of a half-pipe, launch into the air and not come down—if he so decided.

So I followed William Hodge the ten blocks away to his home, a one-story suburban-looking house with a sloping paved driveway. It was only starting to sink in.

"So, what do you think?" he asked.

"About what?"

"About my house?"

"Nice, I guess."

"You see the roof?"

"Yeah."

"The driveway?"

"Yeah."

"The roof is where you start. The driveway is where you land. Point A to Point B."

I scratched my head. I sussed it out. Point A to Point B. I know how insane it sounds, but I was thinking it through. *If it's worth doing, do it. If it's not worth doing, do it anyway.* Low roof. One-story drop right onto a downward sloping driveway. I'd seen something like this in a video once. A major opportunity for an intense drop. You'd just have to lift a little when you left the roof and make sure your back wheels hit the ground before your front wheels.

William brought out a ladder and braced it against the roof. "Are your parents home?" I asked.

"They both work." He climbed the ladder, carrying his bike under one arm. When he got on the roof, he walked the bike to the peak, put on his sunglasses and said, "Now watch this."

He stood on the pedals, let go of the handbrakes and started to roll.

I have to admit that it was beautiful. A boy on a bike in mid-flight right outside the front door to his own home. I expected a thud or a grunt upon landing, but it wasn't like that at all. The rear wheel touched down, and then the front, with immediate forward momentum down the steep driveway. When William approached the road at lightning speed, he applied the brakes and let the rear wheel skid into a controlled slide.

"Amazing," was all I could say.

William walked his bike back up the driveway to me. "Your turn."

If I'd had any second thoughts, they were erased by Hodge's performance. I nodded. I climbed up the shaky aluminum ladder and felt the gritty feel of the shingles under my feet. I looked across the street at the neighbors' houses and saw a man and a woman standing in their front doorway, pointing at me. I wondered if they might call William's parents or even the cops.

I figured now or never.

"Just watch out for the gutter," William yelled up.

I set my board down, held it in place with my foot, and then hopped on and began to roll. I stayed half-crouched until my wheels were off the shingles, and then applied a little upward jump as I ollied slightly, leaving the surface. I was ready to fly.

The only problem was one of my rear wheels caught the dreaded gutter.

My board was slightly off centre as I drifted and dropped. I tried to correct it as I fell through the sky. I thought I had things under control. But I guess I didn't.

As I hit—much harder than I expected— front wheels first, my board was cocked sideways. I was off balance. The front trucks smashed apart as I landed, and ball bearings went flying. And so did I.

My board flew out from under me, and I slammed hard on the driveway. My hip took the worst of it, followed by my shoulder. I rolled and yelped in pain from the fall. When I stopped, I was pretty sure I had broken something. How could I not have?

But as I got to my feet, I discovered I was still in one piece. Oh, I ached all over, and, as I looked up again at the roof, I wondered what I had been thinking.

William was standing by the driveway. He didn't rush over to help me. But he didn't laugh either. "Whoa, dude. That was awesome. I thought you had it for sure. You want to try it again?"

I think he was serious. If I hadn't been in so much pain, I may have gotten angry at him. But then I had thought myself a skate god capable of acid-dropping off a roof. I had no one to blame but myself.

I grimaced as I bent over and picked up what was left of my board. I'd done some serious damage to both sets of trucks and wheels. Not only was my body hurting but my board was messed up. I decided to call it a day.

"See ya 'round," William Hodge said as I hobbled off.

I wondered how Jasmine would react when I told her what I had tried to do. I found that out pretty quickly.

The next day at school, *she* tracked *me* down. I was walking down the hall with my busted skateboard. It didn't work, but I felt naked without it. She came up from behind, put a strong hand on my shoulder and spun me around.

"Are you out of your mind?" she said. Kids stopped and stared at us. Then she looked at my board with the busted wheels.

"You really tried to skate off Hodge's roof, didn't you?" I could tell by the fact that she was nearly screaming that she was not impressed.

I shrugged. "I guess I did."

"Why?"

"Um. It seemed like the thing to do at the time." I hadn't expected I'd have to *explain* why I did it.

"Hodge is a pig. Him and his stupid

bike. I've watched him at the park. He acts like he rules the place."

I don't know why I felt I should defend him, but I heard myself saying, "He's a little rough around the edges, but when you get to know him—"

Jasmine cut me off. "Are you guys friends now?" Oh boy, was she mad.

"Not exactly."

"Well, if you're skateboarding off his roof, you must be pretty tight. You're not a very good judge of character, are you?" And then she turned to walk away. "Good-bye," she said, with her back to me.

I was still only getting to know Jasmine, but she was an important part of my life. I didn't know what to do, but my instinct told me to hang back. Why was she so mad at me anyway?

I stumbled off down the hall with my busted skateboard. The other kids at school treated me like I was invisible, like I didn't matter, and they didn't care. I was getting used to that. She was different.

I spent my life savings getting my skate-board repaired. A couple of days without skating and I was going through with-drawal. I was antsier than ever in school. More distracted.

On Wednesday, I failed to hand in my history homework. On Thursday, I drew a blank in English class when asked to write an in-class essay on "Why Poetry is Important" and on Friday, I flunked a math test. Back in Willis Harbor, teachers would take pity on me and give me extra help after school, or, in some cases, give me a passing grade just so I could move on. Here at Random, it wasn't going to be that easy.

It was a bad week all around.

But when Sunday morning rolled around, I jumped out of bed, skipped breakfast and cruised down to the skate park with my new wheels. It was empty. No Jasmine. And the place was full of broken glass. It looked like some creeps had been drinking there the night before and just broke their beer bottles. Jagged chunks of glass were everywhere.

I was about to leave, but I couldn't face sitting at home on a Sunday morning. So I grabbed a plastic bag from the garbage can and I started picking up the glass.

I tried singing a couple of Dead Lions tunes, but I couldn't remember the words. I tried focusing on what I'd have to do this coming week to get my grades up, but that only made me feel worse. And then I thought about my mom. Something about picking up broken glass made me think about her. I'd put her out of my head for the most part. She'd left us, and we were on our own. She was working on a new life far away, and I might never see her again. I felt rotten that there was nothing I could do to pull my family back together.

And that's when the tears came. I was kneeling now, picking up the smaller shards of glass, realizing I'd never get this place safe to skate on. There were too many fragments. I started to raise my hands to wipe my eyes but stopped. My fingertips were bleeding, and I had tiny slivers of glass stuck in them.

That's when I heard skateboard wheels. Someone approaching the park. I looked up, my face still wet from tears, my vision blurred. And I saw her.

Jasmine. On her skateboard. With a broom in her hands.

chapter seven

"Quinn, are you okay?" Jasmine asked. And then she saw my bleeding fingers. And the fact that I was crying. "Don't touch your face."

I can't imagine how pathetic I looked. And I was feeling so humiliated that Jasmine was seeing me like this. I'd hit an all-time low. But then an amazing thing happened. Jasmine set her skateboard down and walked over to where I was kneeling on the pavement. She took my face into her hands in a very gentle way and wiped away the tears. I closed my eyes.

Time stopped. I think I slipped off into some other dimension. I was in free flight. Weightless. Drifting through sky.

As she pulled away, I opened my eyes and stood up. She seemed embarrassed. We both were suddenly shy and awkward. I tried to say something. Anything. But I didn't have a single word to utter.

Jasmine focused on my bleeding fingertips. She led me to the drinking fountain and washed them until the glass slivers were gone. There was some blood, but the cuts were tiny and the bleeding had stopped.

"Bet they don't trash the skate park back in Willis Harbor," she finally said, still sounding shy and uncertain.

"No skate park to trash."

She looked back at the glass at the bottom of the half-pipe and in the bowl. "This really makes me sad."

My own sadness had disappeared. Jasmine had taken care of that.

"Why were you crying?" she asked.

"I was crying?" I was going to pretend that had not been happening. But I wasn't a very good actor.

"Yes."

So I told her about leaving Willis Harbor and how poorly I was doing in school and about my mother.

"My mother died when I was seven," she said. "Sometimes I can't remember what she looked like. And then my grandmother died a year after that."

"I'm sorry."

She smiled a little then. "Do you know how pathetic you looked kneeling on the pavement with all that broken glass?"

"Pathetic is good, right?"

"In this case, yes."

So she told me more about losing her mother and growing up with a father who could never get over the loss of his wife. "There were women who came and went. Each tried to be a part-time mother, but it never worked. It wasn't their fault."

"And now?"

"Now I'm realizing nothing can change the past. And I need to get on with my life."

"What do we do now?"

She took a deep breath and grabbed the broom leaning by the trash can. "We clean up this place so we can skate. It's Sunday, remember? It's *our* time."

As we worked, I told her about my life back in the Harbor, where I learned to skate on the only paved road that passed through the place. She seemed to like hearing about my old home, so I told her one of my favorite stories.

"I remember one foggy morning, I was ripping downhill in a total, flat-out speed session. Then, out of nowhere, there's a big buck deer with a huge rack of antlers standing on the road in front of me. He's looking at me trying to figure out what I am, I guess.

"The deer wasn't expecting a kid on a skateboard to come racing out of the fog.

I didn't know what to do. And neither did the deer.

"When you're going that kind of speed, you can't carve on the board and siphon off much energy. You could scream, of course. And I did that. I decided to crouch down on my board and put my hands over my head. I'm not sure why. Maybe I thought I could go *under* the belly of the deer."

"You're making this up, right?" Jasmine asked.

"No way. It's true. Heck, I figured I was going to just plow into this wonder of nature. And then this amazing thing happened.

"Just as I was about to collide with Mother Nature herself, the deer leaped over me. I tilted my head up to see him flying over me. And I do mean flying. That deer was getting some serious air. And then he was gone.

"I lost it at that point, of course, my mind blown by a skateboarding miracle. I saw the headlights of a car coming up the hill. Time to bail. There was really only one option. The drop-off into the ditch along the road. I slam-dunked into the mud and water."

Jasmine didn't say a word. She just laughed and tapped me with her elbow. "Come on. Let's get back to work."

It was almost noon before we had the place safe to skate on. We got on our boards, and it was different this time. We *owned* the place. And when we skated together, we were in sync. We were working with each other, not competing. It was like a dance. It felt like nothing I'd ever experienced.

And that's when it dawned on me that I was in love.

We only had the place to ourselves until about twelve thirty, and then Hodge and a bunch of bikers arrived. The spell was broken, but we'd had our time.

chapter eight

My mom called again when my dad wasn't home. This time she wanted to talk to me.

"I miss you, Quinn. I wish we weren't so far apart."

I missed her too. It hurt. But I was still mad at her. "You're the one who moved away," I blurted out.

"I know. But I had to leave. I was dying back there."

"It wasn't Dad's fault the fish plant closed."

"I know that too. But it wasn't just that. It was everything."

"Was it really that bad?"

"For me it was. I'd lived there all my life. I raised you. I worked at the crummy restaurant. I hated it."

That last bit hurt. I was silent.

"I didn't hate you. I love you. And I think I still love your father. I just did what had to be done."

"Yeah. You left us." My voice was hard.

"I'm so sorry."

"Dad's got a job now. Why don't you come back?"

"I've got to finish my course—another month. And I've already got a job lined up. I'll be able to send you some money. Things have been pretty tight up to now. But up ahead it looks good."

I didn't want her money. "You think you'll be happy out there?"

"I think I could be." Which meant that she was thinking about never coming back. Until then, I believed she'd finish the course and move back. Now it was starting to sink in.

"Do you miss Willis Harbor? Do you miss the sea?"

"Sometimes." She didn't sound convincing. I was fairly certain I'd lost my mother for good. But the anger had all drained out of me.

"I just wish things could be like they used to be," I said, my voice sounding weak.

"I know, Quinn."

"Bye, Mom."

"Bye. I'll talk to you again soon. I promise."

And I hung up.

I called Jasmine, and I told her about my phone call. I don't usually open up to anybody about my personal life. But this was different. Jasmine was different.

"Can you take me to that town where you grew up?" she asked.

"You really want to go?"

"Yes. Will you take me?"

"Absolutely. We'll take the bus there Saturday." And then it dawned on me. "Oops. I forgot. I don't have any money. I used every cent I had fixing my skateboard."

"Which is why you should not skateboard off people's roofs. It doesn't matter though. I'll pay."

"You will?"

"Sure. Girls pay for some things. You give me the tour, I'll pay the fare."

"Cool."

chapter nine

Saturday was a bright warm day. The bus was crowded, but we found two seats together near the back. We both had our skateboards. People stared at us as we went down the aisle. Funny how older people think that anyone with a skateboard is a troublemaker. I just don't get it.

"This is like an adventure," Jasmine said, sitting down beside me.

"It's like going back to my past," I said.

"I haven't been back home since we moved to the city."

She smiled. The bus began to pull out of the station as she put her hand on my arm and leaned against me. If I had been carrying any troubles in my head, they immediately vanished.

"Ever wonder what it would be like to skate on the moon?" she asked.

"What?"

"Think about it. The moon. Not the dusty part but some place solid. You'd have such low gravity, you'd get major air."

"I never thought about it. But isn't it the gravity that gives you speed? You go down and then you go up, using momentum?"

Jasmine looked surprised. "Yeah, you're right. I hadn't really thought about it that way." She was about to say something else— something like, *For a guy who isn't smart in school, you're actually pretty bright.* But she didn't. It just kind of hung in the air.

"What kind of rocks would be on the moon?" I asked.

"I'm not sure. I think there's a lot of nickel."

"No granite?"

"I don't think so."

"Today, I get to show you granite. Today, I show you what it's like to *skate* on granite."

The bus dropped us off on the hill by the main road. We walked down the turnoff that led to Willis Harbor. In the distance you could see the sea sparkling in the sunlight.

Jasmine seemed dazzled by how beautiful it was. "This is amazing."

We were back in my world now. A powerful mix of so many emotions swept through me that I felt dizzy. I was home.

Just then, a truck came up behind us. It was loud—no muffler. I recognized the sound. It was Reggie, an old fisherman friend of my father's. I turned and waved as he approached. The truck roared to a stop.

"Quinn," he said. "Good to see you, lad. Hop in."

I smiled at Jasmine to let her know it was okay. We opened the squeaky door and got into the truck. The truck smelled like oil and exhaust and fish. Without me asking, Reggie stopped in front of my old house, and we got out.

We said good-bye and stood by the side of the road. The house looked small and empty and sad. There was a For Sale sign in the front lawn. "This is where I grew up," I said.

"Can we go in?"

"No," I said. "Maybe some other time. This isn't what I brought you here for. C'mon."

I led her to the church first. As we walked up the front steps, she looked puzzled. "It's a church," I said. "It's the only one here. I thought we should get married."

She looked totally stunned.

"Just kidding," I said and laughed.

"Do people have weddings here?"

"Sure. My parents got married here." But as soon as I said it, I wished I hadn't.

"Watch this," I said. I dropped my board, pushed for a blast of speed on the top smooth surface, lifted and took the rail for a perfect board-slide down the full length and then a short drop to the sidewalk below.

"You ever get hurt doing that?"

"Lots of times."

"But you didn't give up?"

"Never." And with that, I ran up the steps and did it all over again.

"You only have to fall four hundred and fifty three times before you get it right. It just takes practice," I said.

"You counted how many times you wiped out?"

"I think I had a new scar for each time. That's how I kept count."

The door to the church opened then, and Reverend Darwin walked out. "I thought I heard a familiar sound," he said.

"Reverend Darwin, this is Jasmine."

He smiled at Jasmine. "Welcome. You know Quinn taught me that miracles can happen. He proved that he could defy the laws of physics right before my eyes."

The door to the church was open now, and you could see the sunlight streaming in through the stained glass windows. "Can we go in?" Jasmine asked.

"Of course," the minister said. "Anyone can go in any time. The doors are never locked."

We walked inside. Jasmine was blown away by the quiet beauty of the sanctuary. "It's so beautiful," she said.

"And so empty," the reverend added. "We barely had twenty people here last Sunday. Would you like some tea?"

"Sure," she said.

And we were led to the office in the back where Reverend Darwin made us tea. He and I reminisced about "the good old days," before the town began to die. When we left, I felt both calm and sad. I made one final board-slide down front, with Reverend Darwin in attendance, and I led Jasmine down to the shore.

chapter ten

"I think I'd like to live in a place like this," Jasmine said.

"Most people want to move away from here. Looks like most people *have* moved away from here." There were way more empty houses than I'd expected.

"It's like going back in time," she said.

"And that's a good thing?"

"Yeah. It's a real good thing. I love everything about this place."

When she said that, it made me feel good because I knew that it wasn't just that she liked the town. She liked where I had come from.

We followed the footpath out of the village and through a grassy field. "And now for the main event," I said. "Close your eyes."

She closed her eyes, and I led her further along the path until we came to the rocks. The Ledges. The ultra-smooth, sea-sculpted, rock formation by the ocean. "Open," I said.

When she opened her eyes, she blinked a couple of times, and then she understood why I had brought her here.

"This is where I learned to skate," I said.

Parts of the Ledges were smooth and slick and rounded with small hills and valleys. Other parts were layered and, in places, looked like steps. Some parts of the formation looked like waves. The water at the base of the rocks was dark blue. It was a calm day, and small waves lapped at the rocks.

"I love it," Jasmine said. "But how did

you learn to skate here?" She looked at the water below.

"I lost my first two boards. Then I started using a leash. Then I got good and didn't need a leash."

"But you never ended up in the water?"

"Well, I did. A couple of times. But it kept me humble. Once the waves were kind of big and the water was freezing. But I got out. I learned my lesson."

"Which was?"

"Not to fall into the water." I didn't say another word. I just tossed my board and shot off across the higher flat part of the rock face. I hit the Ledges at break-neck speed and took them like the steps of the public library back in the city. Then I dropped down onto the smooth rounded granite, kicking for air over the little moguls that were made by Mother Nature.

Finally, I dropped low across the front, the ultra-smooth sloping face of rock that was like a wave. I carved a wide powerful arc as I dropped. Jasmine must have thought

I was about to plunge into the sea. But I knew just where to make my bottom turn. If I did it on a wet patch or anywhere with slimy green, I'd lose it, but I'd done this hundreds of times before. There were gritty patches where the wheels grabbed as if they were on concrete.

I cranked the bottom turn and raced back towards the top. Then I did a one-eighty at the top and retraced my path. I was breathing hard when I finally came to a stop in front of Jasmine. I felt only a little guilty about showing off.

"Now my turn," she said.

I wasn't expecting that. "Um. Are you sure?"

"Yes. Tell me what I need to know."

"Well, for your first time, stay high. Work those little slopes in the rocks and don't go for the big rock face. It's not gonna feel like concrete. It's smoother in some places and rougher in others. And there are cracks to watch out for. Just keep some speed and control and let the rocks teach you. I'll stay below in case you lose it."

There was a determined look in her eyes. I was hoping she'd play it conservative.

She did at first, but then she got more adventurous. She dipped down the sloping rock wave once, then twice, then a bit further. That's when she hit one of the wet spots and lost her board. She fell onto the granite, and I had to make a dive for the board before the waves got it.

After that, she let the rocks teach her where to speed up and where to slow down. Before long she had it wired. I'd never seen anyone learn so fast.

I didn't skate alongside her at all. I stayed below, ready to assist, but I wasn't needed. Then I went back up top to join her.

"How was it?" I asked, knowing that she'd just had an amazing session.

"Like skateboarding on the moon," she said. "Only better."

chapter eleven

I think it's safe to say that everyone who saw Jasmine and me after that day knew we had a *thing* going on. This was all new territory to me. I actually looked forward to going to school.

Jasmine started coming over to my house to help me with my homework. She had a way of explaining things that made sense. And when I didn't know what to write my English research paper on, she suggested

I write it on the history of skateboards. The girl was brilliant.

"You should be a teacher," I told her.

"I want to teach geology at university," she said. "And I'll get to travel and do research."

"Maybe find real gold, huh?"

"All you need to know is where to look."

"Think there's gold in those rocks at Willis Harbor?"

"For sure," she said. "We already found it."

I woke up one Saturday morning and discovered my dad hadn't left for work. He was sitting in the kitchen with his hands wrapped around a mug of coffee, staring at the refrigerator.

"Dad, you okay?"

"No."

"What is it?"

"I lost the job."

I'd never seen him look so down.

"They were a little slow getting around to that background check. The criminal record thing."

"But you never committed any crimes."

He scratched his unshaved jaw and put his hands in the air. "When I was twenty-one, I got into a fight with this older man, Harve Boyle. He'd been beating his cat with a stick. I made him stop, and the cat ran off. Then he took a punch at me. I fought back. Not much came of it, except that he called me all kinds of names and we got a couple of swipes in at each other.

"But later, the police came, and I was charged with assault. I had to go to court. Harve told the judge that I had threatened him and tried to injure him. His wife claimed to have seen the whole thing."

"But that's not fair."

"Who ever said life was fair?"

"You did. And so did Mom, that's who."

He nodded. "Yeah. I forgot. I guess we wanted life to be fair. Anyway, I was found guilty, but the judge knew that Harve had a reputation as a nasty character. So I just got a slap on the wrist."

"And a criminal record?"

"Bingo."

"Can't you explain that to them at the police station?"

"I have an appeal in, but it doesn't look good."

"Now what?" I asked.

"I don't know," my father said, looking totally defeated. "I just don't know."

I heard him on the phone that night. It was the first time he had called her. He was in his bedroom with the door closed, so I guess he didn't want me to hear. They talked for a really long time.

I was trying to study for a history test, but I was getting all those nineteenth-century wars mixed up. I couldn't figure out who was fighting who over what. I'd read a page and then not remember a single thing. All I could tell you is that the

War of 1812 probably took place in 1812.

I'd read about at least a dozen wars befor
the phone call was over. Then there was a
tap at my door. My dad walked in.

"I've been talking to your mother," he
said in a low voice.

"How is she?"

"She's good."

"You told her you lost the job?"

"Yep."

"How did that go?"

"She said that she feels bad about that.
Then she said she still loves me. And you
too."

"I knew that," I said. "On both counts."

"And so we talked." He was stalling. The
room was deathly silent.

I closed my history book. "Yeah?"

"Well, your mother and I think it might
be best if we move out there to join her."

I had not seen that coming. "You want us
to move out west?"

"For now, yes. She says I'll have no
problem getting a job. Maybe even train

in the same course she's taking. She'll be finished in a couple of weeks and working. I'll go to that school, work a little on the side, and pretty soon, we'll both have good jobs. We'll be able to buy a nice house."

"Where?"

"Wherever," he said, looking at the floor.

I almost blurted it out. *No way. I refuse to move.* But I didn't. I knew what my father was going through, and I'd cut him a tiny bit of slack for now.

"But I'm happy here now. Things are looking good," I said.

"I know. You've got a girlfriend."

"And I'm starting to feel like I belong here."

"I know that too. Just think about it for now, okay?" And he left.

I wanted to scream. The walls were closing in. I had to get out of there. I put on my jacket and shoes, grabbed my board and went outside.

It was dark, chilly and damp. The

streets were mostly empty. I tossed my
board down and began to cruise along
the sidewalk, dodging a few pedestrians.
I thought about going to see Jasmine.
She'd invited me over a couple of times.
She wanted me to meet her father. But
I had chickened out. No, I wouldn't go
over there tonight.

I headed to the skate park. I'd heard it
was a tough place at night. No little kids
banging their boards around the kiddie
bowl. No daytime regulars. Just a whole
other scene. Kids with pellet guns. Drug
deals. It's one of the reasons that some
people had proposed taking a bulldozer
to the skate park.

I'd never seen the place with lights
before. It had a steely cold feel to it. It
felt like a different place altogether, a
place where bad things happened.

Some older kids were skating the pipe.
And at least a dozen older guys and
girls—nineteen, maybe twenty years old—
were sitting on the benches and on the

concrete, drinking from cans and passing around a bottle. Nighttime at the skate park.

The three guys skating stopped and joined the others, slugged back from the cans. Laughed and hooted.

I cruised over to the half-pipe and noticed broken glass at the bottom again. It wasn't hard to figure out where that came from. Like before, there were jagged chunks of bottles, but the other guys skating hadn't bothered to clean it up. Heck, maybe they were the ones who busted the bottles.

chapter twelve

Just go home, the voice in my head said. But then someone cruised past me on a skateboard and jabbed me in the ribs as he went by. He had a hood up, and I couldn't see his face. With a few swift kicks, he was up the wall and making a one-eighty turn at the lip, and then dropping a gloved hand to graze a turn and avoid connecting with the glass in the pit. He popped back and forth a couple of times, and then raced straight toward me, hood still low over his eyes, like he was some kind of phantom.

I thought he was going to plow right into me, but I held my ground.

He came to an abrupt stop inches from my face, kicked his board up into his hand and popped the hood down. Hodge. His breath smelled funny. I think he'd been drinking beer.

"Hey, Freak. I figured this was past your curfew," he said.

"I don't have a curfew," I said. I pointed to his board. "I thought it was strictly bikes for you. I didn't know you skated."

"Only at night when the little weasels have all gone home and there's elbow room." He paused. "One on one?" he asked.

"What do you mean?"

"We got the pipe to ourselves. You follow me. Then I follow you. Move for move. See who loses it first."

"What about all that crap at the bottom?"

"It makes things more interesting."

I shook my head no.

"C'mon. We can bet on it. Twenty bucks."

Leave it to Hodge to turn it into a contest. "Na."

"Look at it this way: I'll probably lose. The bike is my thing. I just skate as a sideline. You are the full-meal deal. You skate all the time. You've got the advantage." He had that devilish grin again, the one that had prompted me to skate off his roof.

I had come here to skate, to get my mind off that phone call. I couldn't go home. "What the heck," I said. "Sure."

"You first."

The crowd on the sidelines was watching as I pulled up into the pipe. Hot on my heels was Hodge, move for move. He'd obviously done this before. I dropped in, skittered over some of the smaller chunks of glass, rolled up the other side and took my first bite of air. Hodge was right behind, making contact with the wall just inches behind me. The next time I took the wall, I felt something not quite right, tiny particles of glass had embedded into my wheels. Each time I tried to turn, there'd be a hard spot where the wheels would lose their grip and slide. Not good. I eased up a bit. Hodge noted that I was on cruise control. And then we stopped at the top, both of us kicking our boards up high into the air and catching them.

"Quite the circus act," he said, breathing hard. "But that was just warm up, right?"

I remembered the bet. Twenty bucks. Twenty bucks that I didn't have. "See those guys?" He pointed to the older drinking crowd—our audience. "They got money on this too. They know who you are. They've seen you. Some think you're good. Some think I'm good. Whoever wins, some of them are happy. Whoever loses, some of them are not so happy."

"I'm out," I said. "I don't skate for money, and I don't want people betting on me. This sucks."

He shrugged. "Then pay up. I'll explain that you wimped out."

I could see I was in a no-win situation. I felt trapped. "Okay, your turn," I said.

That devil smile again. I tried to pick the glass out of my wheels, but he was already off. I was the dogman this time. Hodge knew how to work me. He made it easy at first, slow and graceful moves, some rail-slides across the lip, some full-on drops, not connecting until halfway down and always avoiding the worst of the jagged glass. We went on like that for about ten minutes. I could sense he was getting tired. I was thinking I might win after all.

And then he misjudged. His trucks caught on the lip and he lost it. I watched the shock on his face as his feet lost his board, and then he was falling backwards down into the pit. His shoulder bounced him once, and then he rolled onto a broken bottle.

I was already down onto a cleaner part of the bottom of the pipe, so I kicked my board up and ran over to him. There was blood on the ground. He was lying on his back. The look on his face said he was in pain.

"Someone call an ambulance," I yelled to the older guys. But they were getting up to split. No one seemed to be in the mood to be a Good Samaritan.

A police car had just driven up onto the edge of the skate park.

Hodge let out an unearthly howl. He was in serious pain.

Two police officers came running over. I think they believed we'd been in a fight. Maybe they thought I'd knifed Hodge.

"Stand back and don't move," one shouted at me.

"He's hurt," I blurted out. "We were skating. He fell on a busted bottle."

One officer called for an ambulance while the other carefully rolled Hodge over. A chunk of the bottle was lodged in his lower back.

Hodge was crying now. I watched as

they put pressure on the wound without taking the glass out. I felt scared and helpless. And angry at myself for getting lured into a stupid bet.

When they hauled him off in an ambulance, I had no idea how bad the injury was. The cops asked if I wanted a ride home, and I said yes. They were cool enough about it. They said they were sorry about my friend but that we shouldn't be there at night.

My father was sitting on the back steps of the apartment building when we pulled up. One of the cops recognized my father and said, "Oh, he's your son."

"Is he in trouble?" my dad asked.

"No. He's okay," the officer said. "Just happened to be at the wrong place at the wrong time."

chapter thirteen

Later the next day, I made a few phone calls to try to find out what happened to Hodge. The hospital said that he wasn't there. That's all they'd say. I fumbled through the phone book looking at last names until I found a David Hodge and the street name I was looking for. I dialed.

Hodge answered.

"You okay?"

"I'm alive, aren't I? Or do you think you are talking to a ghost?"

Hodge told me that he had been badly cut and lost some blood. They had to stitch him up, and he'd probably be proud of the scar for the rest of his life. But there wasn't any real damage. He'd think twice before making bets again and doing something stupid like that. Or maybe not. It's hard to say.

After that, I finally got up the courage to go over to Jasmine's house. I needed someone to talk to. She was home alone, and we sat on her front steps. I told her about the skate park scene, and it seemed to really trouble her. Maybe I should have stopped there, but I went on to tell her about what my dad had said. That we might move out to be with my mother.

"Do you want to move?" she asked.

"No," I said, "of course not. I want to stay here."

"But she's your mother."

"And she was the one who left. I don't

think my dad really wants to go. I think he wants my mom back though. We both do."

"Aren't you mad at her for leaving you?"

I had thought about that a lot. "I don't know. Not really. I think she did what she had to do."

"But your dad can find another job here, can't he?"

I realized, yet again, that I had grown up in a different world from Jasmine. Her father was some kind of businessman. He made good money. "My father worked in a fish plant," I said. "He didn't graduate from high school. He can probably find a job doing something, but it's more expensive living in the city than he thought. We're just scraping by. And now that he's lost his job, it doesn't look good."

"But I don't want to lose you," she said.

It was wonderful hearing her say that. But everything seemed so impossible.

"If you move away, we'll grow apart,

won't we?" she said. "It won't be the same. Everything will change."

Things got pretty sullen after that. We just sat on the steps staring at the traffic, neither one of us speaking. All I could think about was losing her and how bleak the future would be. It was like a heavy metal door shutting on a beautiful part of my life.

Her father pulled in the driveway then and got out. Jasmine introduced me, and I could tell he wasn't impressed. I had a habit of leaving a bad first impression on adults. He asked how I was doing in school and what I wanted to do after high school. I said I didn't know. I hadn't figured it out yet. The end of high school was a long way off.

Jasmine's father looked at his watch, and then, to end the conversation, he said, "Jasmine, you better come in and get ready. We're going out, remember?" He walked inside and closed the door.

"He's got a new girlfriend," Jasmine said.

"He's taking me to a restaurant to meet her. We've been down this road before. He's attracted to very shallow women."

"It must feel strange."

"It does. And he always wants my approval. But I haven't really approved of any of them. I keep hoping one of them will be like my mom. But that's probably impossible, because I don't remember much about her. I have this image in my head and a feeling about what she was like, but she keeps fading. I miss her all the time, and I don't even really remember her. At least your mother is still alive." She sounded very sad now. I understood what she was trying to tell me. I should go out west and be with my mom. *I had to do it.* It was the right thing.

Her father opened the door again. "Jazz?"

"I'm coming," she said and got up and went in.

"Tomorrow's Sunday," I said.

"Yeah." And the door closed.

My mom called that night. She wanted to talk to me again.

"You'll love it out here. You can see the mountains from the city."

That's all she had to offer. Mountains? No ocean?

"It'll be a fresh start for all of us."

"I don't want to start fresh," I said.

"There's a girl, right?"

"Yeah, there's a girl. But it's more than that. I want to finish high school and then move back to the Harbor."

"But it's dying. There's nothing there for us."

"It's changed. But it's my home."

"It *was* a home for all of us. But not anymore."

"I went there with Jasmine. She loved it. It felt so good to be back. At least it's only an hour bus ride away. But if I move away now, I may never come back. I'll lose everything."

"I'm sorry, Quinn. But your father is going to enroll in the program here. While he studies, I'll have a really good job. Do you know how much that means? Pretty soon, we'll both have real jobs. Good pay and steady work."

"How do you know that it's always going to be like that? What if something changes and there's no work?"

She let out a sigh. "Then we cross that bridge when we come to it." She paused. "I'm sorry, Quinn. I know this is hard on you."

"So it's a done deal?"

"We need to do this. For all of us."

I didn't say anything further. I hung up. I felt so frustrated.

And then my father came into my room and said we'd be flying out in a week. "That will give us enough time to settle up some things here. Maybe if I lower the asking price on the old house, we could have some cash."

I know it sounds like a terrible thing to say, but just then, I hated my parents for what they were doing.

Jasmine was not at the skate park Sunday morning. I cruised around for a while, but my heart wasn't into it. I waited for an hour, just sitting on the bleachers hoping she'd show up, but she didn't.

When the little kids started arriving, I was in a foul mood. I went to a pay phone to try to phone Jasmine, but all I got was voice mail. It was starting to sink in. She believed that me having my mother around was more important than anything in the world, and she was willing to let me go. She'd move on.

I sat back down on the bleachers and felt powerless and got angrier by the minute. Finally, I got back on my board and pushed out into the crowd of kids. A few got out of my way. The ones who didn't, I carved around. I went into the bowl first and then into the half-pipe. My rage gave me more speed and power than I'd ever felt before. I pumped hard, threw myself up into the air above the lip and out, dropping like a stone but always connecting with the wall, blasting across the bottom and up the other side.

The kids were smart enough to clear out and let me have it. Anyone seeing me for the first time would have thought I was more than a skate freak. I was a skate terminator.

Gravity fed me, and then on the sweep up, it released me and I soared. Boy with wings. Wingman. The Great Flying Dorf. I kept getting faster and popping higher into the air. A lot of the kids were standing on the sidelines, watching in disbelief.

And then something happened.

I was midair, grasping the back of my board with two fingers, preparing for the drop when it popped into my head. Two words.

Take charge.

It was what skateboarding had taught me. You either let things happen and just cruise along. Or you take charge. And *make* things happen. All my life I'd allowed adults to make decisions about my life. Parents. Teachers. Other adults. Some adult was always in charge. I was just a kid. But when I was on my board, I was responsible for my every move. I felt free and alive— no matter how difficult the situation was. In fact, the more difficult, the better.

All this occurred in a flash. And then I was dropping out of the sky, connecting, arriving at the bottom of the pipe and kicking my board up.

It was time to go home.

chapter fourteen

My father was packing clothes into a couple of old beat-up suitcases when I got home.

"What time is it where mom is?" I asked.

"Three hours earlier. Why?"

"Think she'll be up?"

"Why?"

"Because we need to call her."

He stopped packing. "You still think you can change this, don't you?"

"Let's just call her. Let me talk."

"Quinn. Look, I'm broke. She's sending us money for airfare. I don't have a job. I tried to stay, but it's just not gonna work."

"I need to stay here. I need this for me." I was thinking of Jasmine. I was thinking of leaving Willis Harbor forever and going to the other side of the country. I was thinking about living unhappily ever after.

"I'm sorry, but your mother made the right call. We gotta go. Once we get on our feet out there, we can think about a way to come back."

"But that could take years."

"It might."

"I want to talk her. I want for Mom to see this the way I see it. And I want you to hear it too."

My mother sounded groggy on the other end. It was early out there.

"I have an idea," I said. "It's not perfect. But it's an idea."

She surprised me. She said, "I'm listening."

"Your course is over soon, right?"

"Right."

"And if you came back here with the course completed, you'd get a job, right?"

"I already have a job lined up. Besides the pay is way higher here."

"But so are the living expenses. You said that."

"Well, yeah, but we'd adapt."

"But you could find a job here that you'd be trained for?"

"I think so, yes. But we've already got your father enrolled and in a little while, we'll both have good jobs. It's what we've dreamed of."

It was what my mom had dreamed of, yes. But my dad, he would have been happier in Willis Harbor, working in the smelly old fish plant. He looked at me now, a curious twinkle in his eye. He did not want to leave at all.

To my mom I said, "What if *you* finish your course and *you* come back? We live together while you work and Dad goes out there to take the course."

"But then we'd still not all be together," she said.

"I know, but it would be temporary, right?"

"I guess so. You mean, he'd come back after the course?"

"It's not that long. He'd be back before I was out of school."

My dad had stopped packing the suit-case. He was smiling now.

My mom was hesitant. "It's not at all what your father and I agreed on. How does he feel about this?"

My father said nothing. He just gave me a thumbs-up. "I think I could persuade him."

There was silence on the other end. My father's eyes were tearing up.

"And if we did this," my mom said, "made this sacrifice for you—and it would be a sacrifice—what would you do in return?"

"I'd work my butt off in school. I'd get good grades." These were perhaps the most unlikely words to ever come out of my mouth. All my life I'd been getting Ds and Fs. Sometimes the Ds were gifts from teachers. Now I was promising to get Cs. I could do it if Jasmine helped me. I knew I could.

Both of my parents were stunned. I mean, speechless stunned. I had never, ever in my life played the school card. Now it was out there, I'd have to live up to it. But only if they went for *my* plan.

"Put your father on the phone," my mom said.

I handed Dad the receiver.

"Let's give the boy a chance. Let's do it," he said.

But I knew my mom was already convinced.

It wasn't until spring that Jasmine and I had a chance to return to Willis Harbor. My mom drove us. She and Jasmine had gotten to know each other when Jasmine came over to tutor me. I felt bad that I was so slow, that I took up so much of her study time. But I loved being with her.

My father was having a rough time with his course. He was like me. We weren't the sharpest tools in the shed when it came to classroom learning. But he was going to make it, and he'd return. And then we'd be together again as a family. Things hadn't really worked out yet for my mom. She had a job, but it was an office job. It seemed no one around here was willing to hire a woman to run the big machines. But she said that would change. She wouldn't give up.

Over the winter, Hodge and I had become friends, and that changed both of us. We lost the need to compete with each other at the skate park. We became allies of sorts, even though we never really understood each other.

And he never did pay me the twenty bucks he owed me. But I let that go. Letting things go was one of my lessons. *Hang onto the good stuff. Let the bad stuff go. And don't hold grudges.*

I promised to bring him to Willis Harbor and show him the Ledges. But that was for later.

On this bright but cool spring morning, Willis Harbor looked a little dull, a little worn around the edges. The empty houses, the sad streets. But the sea gleamed in the distance. And I always thought that the sea represented hope.

"I want to live by the sea, someday," Jasmine said.

"Yeah, me too," was my answer as we passed our old house. It looked like it had not been lived in for many years rather than several months.

My mother surprised me by pulling into our old driveway. She got out and unlocked the front door of the house and walked in. Jasmine and I followed.

It was again like going back in time. I led Jasmine up to my old bedroom. The furniture was still there. Dust and spider webs covered everything. She just walked to the window and looked out.

"You can see the ocean from your bedroom. And you can see the rocks."

"That's what I woke up to every day."

"I bet you'd love to move back here right now, wouldn't you?"

"No," I said. "I made this promise about school. And I can't make it work without you."

She nodded. She knew it was true.

We left my mom alone at the house for a while, even though I could tell it wasn't easy on her. We grabbed our boards from the car and headed toward the Ledges.

Some of the rocks were quite wet, so we had to limit ourselves to the higher parts. But the granite felt smoother than ever beneath us. We skated cautiously, but this was somehow more beautiful.

It was a dance, a dance on granite by a fierce blue sea.

And then we walked further out to the point, where the rocks were rough, but you can climb up higher and look further toward the horizon.

"Think you'll really move back here someday?"

"Someday," I said. "But not yet."

When we walked back to the house, my mom was taking the For Sale sign down. Dark clouds were approaching with a new sharp wind off the sea. The day was turning cool and damp. There were rough times ahead for all of us. The gravity of things would pull us down. And there would be walls ahead. But the walls wouldn't stop us. We would use them to blast up into the heights and prepare for the next challenge ahead. Whatever that might be.

Award-winning author Lesley Choyce has written sixty-eight books and is a year-round surfer at Lawrencetown Beach, Nova Scotia.